# REAL ELVES

# REAL ELVES

## An Emily Castles Mystery

HELEN SMITH

TYGER BOOKS

This story first first appeared in the anthology *Naughty or Nice*,
published in aid of Kids Need to Read.
This edition first published by Tyger Books in 2014



A CIP catalogue record for this book is available
from the British Library.

ISBN: 978-0956517081

*For my daughter Lauren*

*and her friend Harry, the former Head Gardener*

# REAL ELVES

"I want you to think of all the ways you could injure a child," said Miranda. She was dressed as an elf. "I mean, really hurt them—not just a bump or a bruise. I'm talking about snapping a limb or bashing in a head, or even"—she lowered her voice—"loss of life."

Emily loved the run-up to Christmas, it was like the start of a poem: spicy cinnamon and glints of gold, green leaves and red robes, fairy lights and children singing. Even in the final scramble, in the week before everything shut down, when people frenziedly bought presents they couldn't afford and drank too much at office parties, she always tried to remain cheerful and calm. Now, standing at the entrance to an enchanted forest, on the third floor of a department store in London, dressed in a red robe with a hood, carrying a wicker basket, she tried to be helpful. "I suppose you could hit them really hard with a cricket bat?"

"I think you misunderstood me," said Miranda. "I'm not suggesting you *deliberately* injure a child. I'm asking you to consider how a child could be injured by accident. In there." She pointed into the dark interior of the forest, where exotic flowers had bloomed overnight, where the gnarled limbs of almost-human trees joined protectively over a meandering pathway that led to Santa's grotto, where gold and silver baubles were strung up among strands of twinkling white lights that threaded through the branches.

"Oh," said Emily. "I see ... Well, could they be electrocuted by the fairy lights? Injured by something falling from a tree?"

Miranda nodded. Emily was on the right track.

As is so often the way in briefing meetings, other members of the staff joined in now they knew what they were supposed to say. Unlike most staff meetings, however, everyone present was dressed as a character from a fairy tale.

Ray—a woodcutter—thought that shards of glass from broken Christmas tree baubles might get embedded in little fingers. He thought that trailing wires from plug sockets might trip tiny feet, or bits of scenery might poke any part of the body, but especially the eyes.

"Yes!" said Miranda. "It's our job to protect them from all that."

Ray adjusted his green felt Robin Hood hat so it sat at a jauntier angle, the pheasant's tail feather stuck in the side of it tickling the ends of his cornrows. Ray was a meaty young man who liked to work out in the gym four times a week. His big brown arms were sinewy and strong; he stood with his thick legs planted wide apart. He looked like a tree that had dressed up as a woodcutter. He shrugged and rolled his mahogany eyes, to show that he didn't consider it *his* job to protect anyone "from all that."

Miranda pretended to be indifferent to his indifference. "Anyone else?"

A centaur called Selena—the lower half horse, the upper half human, despite the long face—thought the children themselves might be the cause of trouble. There was a rumble of dissent from the group, but Selena was adamant. "Seriously, guys, it's nonsense to believe that children are inherently good. They fight and cheat and steal and tell tales."

Emily wondered if Selena wasn't getting children mixed up with cowboys.

"We want the children who pass through the forest to be transformed by the experience—but only in a good way," said Miranda. "That's all I'm saying."

"It would be great if it did transform them," said Selena. "Imagine that. Like, if Santa was real. You bring a few naughty kids and walk them through the forest, Santa has a chat with them, and they come out well-behaved."

"Or politicians!" said Ray. "Or bankers."

"We'd be famous!" said Selena.

Miranda gave herself a little hug. "You know what? When I was at art school, I might have wished for fame—or notoriety. But then I grew up. I've got friends who sell their work for millions. But

I'd much rather spend my time on community projects, summer festivals, a few commercial installations like this one. Because for half an hour or so, as they go through it, the children believe the magic is real. If I could have one wish for all of us, to celebrate our hard work, it would be that—just for one night—we could believe it too."

"I'd rather be rich," said Ray.

"Me too. Sorry," said Selena. "What about you, Emily? What would you ask Father Christmas for?"

"No need to ask," Emily said. "He always brings me the same things: a chocolate orange, a pair of long socks and a puzzle."

Miranda laughed. The group started to pick up their coats and bags to show they were ready to leave. It was so late already.

But Miranda had another strange question before she would let them go. "Do any of you know any children?" She stared beseechingly around the group. She might have been asking, "Do you know anyone from Bhutan?" as if children lived in an isolated kingdom a long, long way away from

London, and it was impossible to meet them under normal circumstances.

"You don't need to worry about finding children to see Santa," said Selena. "The store will do that."

"It's a tradition," said Ray. "People come with their kids year after year. You'll get plenty of bookings."

They were pretending to reassure her, but really they were enjoying the smug feeling that follows the sudden realization that the person in charge is an idiot. It can make a pleasant end to a long day, unless that person is about to lead you into battle from out of the trenches.

Miranda tugged at the sleeves of her green jacket, irritated at their smugness. "Yes. Yes, yes, yes. I *know*. We're fully booked as soon as it opens. But we need a child to test out the forest before then. It seems we've thought of everything, but we won't have. No matter how many times we walk through it, there's always something. You have to have a child to go through it. My niece was going to do it, but she's got chicken pox."

Ray had a suggestion. He bent his knees and hunched down, resting his forearms on his big thighs. "Couldn't we—"

Emily was horrified. *Couldn't we what?* Ray looked as if he was miming using the toilet.

"I know what you're going to say," Miranda held up her hand to cut him off. With a background in set design for the theatre, she was obviously better at interpreting mime than Emily was. "Asking a short person's no good." She sighed with the wearied air of someone who had tried asking short people to test out her Christmas installations many times in the past, and always found them wanting. "Children have a different way of seeing things. So, does anyone know any children?"

As it turned out, the children they knew might as well have been in Bhutan. Selena had a baby, but the baby was too young to test the layout and functionality of the magical forest. The other staff were childless. They had neighbours. But none of the neighbours' children were quite the right age for this project. They had nephews and nieces, but the nephews and nieces were in Cornwall or Dorset or Birmingham or Glasgow.

Emily could see another problem, even if they identified a suitable child to test out the project. "Won't they all be in school? It's Friday tomorrow."

Miranda sighed again—at the selfishness of children, the inflexibility of the British educational system, the stupidity of her staff... Emily wasn't sure exactly. The sigh was all-encompassing. "I think we could write a letter to the school, don't you? An educational visit. Think what the child would learn."

To be fair to Miranda, she was right. Helping to create the magical forest had been the best job Emily had ever had, like a form of extreme gardening. She had learned a lot. For the last five days, all day and late into the night, Emily had worked among craftspeople and technicians hammering, sawing, painting and stitching to create something magical and beautiful. And now it was finished, children would wander along the path that led to Santa, ushered by staff dressed as characters from fairy tales, accompanied by a responsible adult, choosing one piece of gold or silver fruit from the overhanging branches of the trees above the pathway and trading it for a gift from Santa.

Along the way, to keep them entertained, they would pass by oversized musical boxes and cabinets that could be operated when the child turned the handle. The cabinets were filled with all sorts of wonders: dancing automata, films glimpsed through peepholes, shadow puppets, talking birds. Tickets were expensive. The chance to wander through this place, almost alone, for free, would be a wonderful experience for a child of the right age. But where were they going to find that child at such short notice?

"Could we offer a kind of golden ticket?" said Ray. "The kid who wins it gets to come in and explore the forest before it opens."

"No," said Miranda.

Then Emily had a clever idea. One thing you must *never* do at work is have a clever idea. If you do have one, you need to keep quiet until the urge to share it passes. Emily should have known better. She really should. "There's a neighbour of mine, he lives at the end of the street. Harry. He's a retired Head Gardener and we're friendly because he gives me tips on my garden, though I don't know him well. Anyway, he said he doesn't see enough of his granddaughter, Sophie. I'm sure she lives in London. She started school last year so she must be about six years old. At that age, it wouldn't matter much if she missed the last day of term. And Harry would be so pleased if he could spend the day here with her."

"Perfect! You talk to Harry, tell him to ask the parents' permission, find out the name of the school. Call me tonight, OK? We open on Saturday, so this has to happen tomorrow. I'll write an e-mail to the head teacher and tell her Sophie needs to have the afternoon off. It's a win for everyone. Sophie and Granddad get a tour of the forest; we show them how we transformed this place, and how this place can transform two ordinary people into two adventurers exploring an enchanted forest. We get a dress rehearsal. They get a magical experience, and they get to spend time together. What could go wrong?"

With all permissions duly granted, the next day Harry collected his granddaughter from school just after lunch and brought her to Oxford Street on the 137 bus. They sat at the top at the right-hand side, directly above the driver, and enjoyed a lovely view of London as they made their way through tree-lined streets to the magical place where the branches of the trees were hung with gold and silver baubles.

December in London is not nearly as miserable as January or February. In January and February, the rain is too wet, the air is too cold, and the days are too short. In December, there's a bite of cold in the air, but it's a puppy nipping playfully at your mittened hand, rather than the fully grown savaging of the later months. And when it's sunny in December, London's beauty sparkles. That day, as Harry and Sophie travelled on the bus through London together, it was sunny.

Sophie didn't talk much, so Harry talked. He pointed out places of interest: Battersea Park, with its Peace Pagoda, its boating lake and its fragrant rose garden; Chelsea Physic Garden, created by apothecaries in the seventeenth century to grow medicinal plants; Marble Arch with its nose-diving horse head statue; and Tyburn Covent with its enclosed order of nuns. He reminisced about what London was like in the old days, when he was a boy.

The red buses didn't have a door on the back—you could jump on and jump off at any point along the route, although you weren't supposed to. He remembered running after a bus through the traffic with his two best friends, racing to catch up with a bus, jumping aboard and getting told off by the conductor. And, of course, you could smoke upstairs on the top deck. Everything he described sounded so wicked and wrong and old fashioned, as if people back then were trying to harm themselves deliberately. Could Sophie even understand what he was talking about?

But she listened solemnly and nodded. A couple of times she said, "I'd like to do that!"

He wondered if she meant she'd like to run through moving cars to jump onto a bus, or jump off into the traffic. Or was it the smoking she liked the sound of? He wouldn't get many more opportunities to spend time with Sophie if she went back to her mother and told her that. Fortunately, the excitement of a stroll through the magical forest and meeting Santa should give her plenty of positive things to talk about when she got back home.

Emily was waiting for them when they arrived. So was Miranda. Emily was dressed in her red, hooded cape. Miranda was dressed in a green tunic, green pointed shoes, green tights and false ears. She was accompanied by a large poodle whose fur had been styled to make him look like a reindeer. He was wearing antlers and an embroidered saddle. Miranda was carrying an aerosol can of cinnamon-scented spray.

"Is that your poodle?" Emily asked her as they waited.

Miranda gave the air an excited squirt of cinnamon. "Use your imagination! He's not a poodle. He's a reindeer."

An elderly, creaky-looking man with rheumy blue eyes approached them, with a small, blond child of about six years old.

Miranda whispered, "Showtime!"

Emily was to greet each child in a warm and friendly manner, ask the name and confirm the spelling with the adult accompanying them, then write the name on a sticky label and press it firmly to the child's coat, on the left-hand side near the shoulder. This would allow Father Christmas to greet the child by name, giving the illusion that he had been keeping up with their good deeds and misdemeanours. It would remind the responsible adult accompanying the child that they were not anonymous. The name would be checked off against a list of prebooked tickets. There was no readmission.

So this was the procedure Emily followed now. She greeted Harry and asked his granddaughter her name. Harry touched the little girl lightly on the shoulder, to get her attention—his hands were knobbly with rheumatism.

The little girl had been petting the reindeer poodle, but she stopped and gave her name. "Sophie."

Emily wrote the name on a label and stuck it to the child's coat. From a basket on the table next to her, Emily took a sealed letter addressed to Father Christmas, which was to be delivered by the child to the woodcutter. This letter allowed entry to the forest.

There would be several woodcutters dotted around the forest. Their job was to help the young child remove the dangling bauble once they had selected it from whichever branch of whichever tree they wanted—and, of course, ensure that only one was taken.

"It's difficult to see woodcutters as heroes, isn't it?" said Miranda, as they watched Sophie hand over her letter to Ray. "With deforestation and everything."

From deep within the forest, they heard the sound of Santa trying out the acoustics in his grotto. "Ho ho ho!"

Miranda rolled her eyes. "Sounds like a drunken uncle at a family gathering—not even a proper uncle, a former neighbour that everyone calls uncle out of respect, and now the respect has gone. I didn't want Santa, to be honest. A whiskery old man squatting in the middle of my forest asking impertinent questions of children about their behaviour. What's that all about? I'd much rather have had a Fairy Godmother. But the store owners insisted. Do you think little Sophie will choose a gold bauble or a silver bauble?"

"Gold? I don't know."

"There's a perceived difference in value, but the gifts all cost about the same, of course. I'm doing a study to see how the choices break down on gender lines. Do you know the most useful thing I learned when I was at art college?"

Emily tried to remember the most useful thing Miranda had taught her over the past few days. "Welding?"

"How to apply for funding. I should get a little extra money from a university for this study. You want to come to the security booth? You can meet my godmother."

Miranda had a fairy godmother?

"She'll be watching the CCTV to make sure my study's set up properly."

Miranda had a fairy godmother who kept watch on people via CCTV? Of course Emily wanted to meet her. She followed Miranda to the security booth.

On the way, Miranda tried to justify the use of cameras. "With the low lighting in the forest, you'd be surprised how many people are tempted to steal—both staff and members of the public. And then there are the various hazards. You'll have children pulling down fairy lights, poking themselves in the eye with sharp objects, walking into walls in the poorly lit grotto, rolling out of control on their wheely shoes. And then there are the pranks. Every year, in a project like this, someone plays some sort of prank. It's not always malicious, but seasonal work attracts disgruntled staff. Students. They think they're better than the job on offer. You know the sort of thing. A partridge in a pear tree replaced by a penguin."

Emily couldn't help it. She giggled.

"And, of course, we have to make sure no child gets separated from its parent. Have you ever lost a child, Emily?"

She hadn't.

"Even if it only happens for five minutes, it's absolutely the worst thing. For those five minutes, you can't promise yourself you'll ever see the child again."

Miranda had that carelessness that often came with creativity. Emily took a moment to wonder how many children she might have lost over the years. Emily had never experienced anything like it herself, but she had seen it happen: the absolute still of the parent, like someone drowning, in the moment when the body shuts down, right before they sink beneath the waves. A few times she had lost sight of her dog, Jessie, in the park, and that had been bad enough. But when she called her, Jessie had always come bounding towards her with her big cheerful golden retriever smile.

"Fortunately, in all the years I've been doing these things, I've only ever witnessed a happy outcome. The moment when the little lost hand of the child touches their parent's and everything's OK... It's almost worth losing one in the first place, just to see that happen. Almost. But we're so well set up in here, with the cameras and the fairy-tale characters chaperoning them through the forest. They're not out of sight even for a moment. It's not going to happen."

When they reached the security booth, Emily was delighted to see that Miranda's "fairy godmother" was her old friend Dr. Muriel, a middle-aged professor who lived across the road from her in Brixton.

Dr. Muriel was delighted to see Emily, too. "I'm helping Miranda with her bauble project. She planned the forest, she built it, she's running it, and she's even managed to wring some funding from the university for this study. If this project had been a pig, she'd have found a way to eat the whole thing," she said proudly. "What are you up to? Are you investigating something? Don't tell me there's going to be a murder!"

"There won't be a murder," said Emily. "It's Christmas."

They settled down to watch Harry and Sophie explore the forest, guided by Ray. Miranda was excited as she explained what she had created to Dr. Muriel. "We've got simple things dressed up to look complicated. Duplicates. Mirrors. Shadows. Optical illusions."

They watched Sophie visit Santa. He was sitting in a honeycomb-shaped, dimly lit grotto on a large, red velvet throne. Naturally he was wearing a red robe and whiskers. He had a computer in front of him on a gold table shaped like a sleigh. The back of the computer screen had been embedded in a glittery white snow globe.

"Ho ho ho! Hello, Sophie. What would you like for Christmas?"

She thought for a few moments, then said, "Something so I can do gardening."

"Aw," said Emily in the security booth.

"Have you been good this year, Sophie?" Santa asked. "I'd better just check my records." He typed on the keyboard in front of him and peered at the screen. "Yes. Very good. Don't forget to choose one of the baubles from the trees on your way out. Open it up; you'll need to show what's written inside to the elves. Perhaps Granddad can help with the reading?"

"Are they real elves?" Sophie asked.

"Well," Santa said cautiously, "I can't say for certain. They look real enough to me. Of course, looks can be deceiving."

"Do they do elf things?"

"Yes. Well, they hand over presents to children out the back there."

Sophie nodded, satisfied. "They must be real elves."

For a moment, Emily lost sight of Sophie. But then there she was, standing next to Santa. Harry was standing behind them.

"Shall we take a photo, then?" Santa prompted.

Ray picked up a bakelite camera as big as an encyclopedia, with a grapefruit-sized silver disc surrounding the flashbulb on top. The three of them blinked as he took the picture. Ray stepped back, wincing.

"That's going to get annoying," said Dr. Muriel.

"I'll see if he can't adjust the settings on that piece of kit—modern technology in old-fashioned housing, it's easy enough to do. This is why we need a dress rehearsal before the crowds come in." But Miranda seemed pleased with the way it was going. "You see all that business with the computer screen? He wasn't really checking whether or not she'd been good."

"I should think not," huffed Dr. Muriel.

"He makes a note of the gift the child says they'd like and e-mails it to the elves waiting at the back, so they can get it prepared. We've got the timing right, I think, though it's a bit tight."

They watched as Harry and Sophie made their way out of the forest. Along the way, almost at the very last tree, Sophie stopped and pointed to a gold bauble. Ray used his plastic axe to help her snare it from the branch.

"Aha!" said Dr. Muriel. "Gold. Very good."

"Is it significant, do you think?" Miranda asked her.

"I don't know. Is it?"

Harry opened the bauble and read the number written inside. "Seventy-two," he said, peering at it in the darkness with his glasses. "What do you suppose you'll get, then, Sophie?"

She shrugged.

"So it doesn't matter what the number is?" Dr. Muriel asked Miranda.

"Exactly! It's misdirection. Harry and Sophie will make their way to the edge of the forest, and Sophie will trade in her bauble to collect a gift from the elves. And it will seem amazing to her—and to most of the adults, I guarantee you—that whatever bauble she chose has a number inside that matches so closely the gift she told Santa she wanted. It doesn't even matter if a child asks for a puppy and gets a toy one. The magic of it, the way someone seems to have *listened*, the way the child herself is in control of the outcome because of the choice she's made, it's enough to make them feel very happy. You know, if this study goes off OK, Aunt Muriel, I'd be happy to come along to the university to do a talk about it."

But Miranda's self-congratulatory daydreaming was interrupted by a phone call.

"There's a problem," she said. "We need to go down there."

"What is it?" said Emily. "Is Harry all right?" Maybe the excitement had been too much for him.

"Come and see," said Miranda. She looked alarmed—frightened, even, as she led the way to the elves' station at the back of the forest.

"I'd like to report a missing child," said Harry when they got there.

"What do you mean?" said Emily. "Which child?"

He indicated Sophie. "This child."

"She's standing right next to you!" said Miranda. "She's not missing!"

"This isn't the child I came in with." Harry adjusted his glasses. "She looks like Sophie. But this isn't Sophie."

A small crowd had gathered. Ray was there. Selena was there. Dr. Muriel, Emily and Miranda were there. There were gasps when they heard what Harry had to say.

"You're confused, Harry," said Miranda. "It happens to the best of us. I look at my own face in the mirror some days, I hardly recognise it."

"What's your name, dear?" Dr. Muriel asked the child.

"Sophie."

Sophie was wearing the sticky label Emily had written for her. She looked exactly the same, except that she was carrying a cardboard box with a picture of a plant pot with a gaudy red amaryllis flowering in it, and she had a utility belt around her waist kitted out with small-sized gardening tools, including a trowel and a fork—the elves had done their job well this afternoon. The amaryllis was a particularly good choice. Strong green shoots would start growing from the bulb almost as soon as Sophie took the pot out of the box and watered the soil. Emily knew because she used to get one from her grandmother every year when she was around the same age. Wait! Why was she suddenly thinking about her grandmother? Emily drew her red cloak around herself and shivered, spooked at the recollection of such an old memory.

Dr. Muriel continued with her gentle questioning. “And is this your grandfather, Sophie?”

Sophie shook her head. “No.”

There was a lot of murmuring from the crowd at that. “No!” “No?” “She said no!”

Sophie seemed upset that anyone would doubt her. “You can ask Santa, he knows me. I haven’t got a granddad.”

“She’s been substituted!” whispered Selena. “Aliens or... or some mischievous spirit dematerialized the child while she was in the forest, and put back one that was the same size, but slightly different.”

“I think there’s probably an easier explanation,” said Dr. Muriel. “What do you think, Emily? You’re good with puzzles.”

“They’re twins,” suggested Ray.

“Both called Sophie?” said Dr. Muriel.

Ray shrugged. “It’s a popular name.”

Dr. Muriel didn’t know whether to be exasperated or entertained. “Now, Ray, it really would be a failure of imagination for parents of twins to name both of them Sophie."

"I'm sure this is the little girl Harry came in with," said Emily. "She looks exactly the same. That's my handwriting on the label on her coat."

Miranda said, "Sophie, do you remember seeing a reindeer when you came in?"

Sophie placed her amaryllis-in-a-pot on the floor next to her, carefully. She folded her arms and shook her head.

"Oh, this is awful," wailed Miranda. "If only my niece didn't have to be in her school play today. This disaster could have been avoided. It'll be all over the papers if we've lost a child here."

Emily was suddenly suspicious. Miranda couldn't have staged this for the notoriety she said she'd grown out of wanting, could she? "I thought you said your niece had chicken pox?"

"Something like that. School play, chicken pox... I can't remember exactly. I just know it's something that would be intensely irritating if I had to endure it."

"Is this a stunt?" said Emily. "A prank—like substituting the penguin for the partridge in the pear tree?"

"No!" Miranda seemed to be in earnest. "Something like this, it's more than a prank with a penguin, which, I'll admit to you now, *I* carried out. I thought it might be a bonding experience for the staff. This isn't a prank! With a child reported missing, someone will want to call the police, they'll want to take Sophie away—and Christmas will be ruined. Has anyone called them yet? I do hope not. Ray, can you ask security *not* to call the police, please."

"They have to call the police within fifteen minutes if a child's reported missing," said Ray. "It's protocol."

"But she's here! She's right here!" Miranda grabbed hold of the child. "Sophie, you must remember the reindeer."

Sophie said, "I only remember the dog."

"Yes! Yes! You see? It is the same child you came in with, Harry. She remembers the poodle. This is your granddaughter."

"No, she isn't."

"I'm going to call the school, Harry. I'll get Sophie's head teacher on the phone. Maybe she can talk some sense into you."

As Miranda stepped away from the group to call Sophie's head teacher, Emily said, "Sophie looks the same to me. Harry, you're the one who looks different."

"Ooh!" Selena liked that idea.

Miranda, midway through calling Sophie's school, stopped dialling and waved the phone to get Emily's attention. "No! Seriously. One missing person is enough. Don't start with that."

"Did you collect the picture you had taken with Santa?" Emily asked Sophie.

Sophie shook her head. She hadn't.

Emily smiled at her. "I think we should take a look at it."

Selena just about whinnied with excitement. "You think Santa's responsible! That's brilliant. It's got to be him. He did it."

Dr. Muriel didn't share Selena's enthusiasm. "An out-of-work actor in a red robe and whiskers? How?"

Selena looked down, pawing at the ground with her shiny hoof, as if she expected to uncover a clue etched into the vinyl on the floor. Then she tossed her head back. "Magic camera?"

"Ah," said Dr. Muriel politely. "Interesting theory."

"Not as crazy as it sounds," said Ray. "He coulda made the switch when everyone was blinded by the flash." He swung his axe. "You want me to make a citizen's arrest? Hold him 'til the police come?"

"I don't think that will be necessary," said Dr. Muriel, recoiling slightly as Ray brandished the plastic weapon. "If he's guilty of something and he tries to escape, he won't get very far in that getup. The police will easily recognize him."

"How long have we got?" asked Emily. "Until the police are called?"

Ray looked at his watch. "About ten minutes."

"Would you mind getting the photo?" Emily asked him. "The printer's by the elves' station."

"Do you need the ten pounds?" Harry opened his wallet. "I think you have to pay for it."

"It's OK, Harry," said Emily.

"If you get any trouble from the elves, you can tell them you're commandeering the photo," Dr. Muriel said to Ray. "For evidence."

Ray slapped the flat of the plastic axe into the palm of his hand, to show that he was ready to tackle anything, even recalcitrant elves. Off he went to get the photo.

The photo was eight inches by six inches, full colour, in a clear plastic wallet. Ray passed it to Selena. Selena held it up next to Sophie. Same girl. Same face. Selena and Ray seemed disappointed. Selena passed the photo to Emily. She examined it. Santa was sitting in a chair, Sophie at his side, Harry behind them. Sophie looked exactly the same.

"That's the child Harry came in with," said Emily.

But still, something didn't look right to her. Harry was different somehow. "I know what it is! You're not wearing your glasses in the photo, Harry. I don't think you had them on when you came in, either. But you're wearing them now."

Harry removed his glasses. He looked at Sophie. "You look blurrier," he said to her. "More like my granddaughter."

"There we are," said Dr. Muriel. "No harm done. Miranda! We've solved the mystery. This is Sophie—Harry just didn't recognise her because he came out of the forest with his glasses on."

But Miranda walked towards her slowly, carefully, as if the ground was giving way beneath her feet. Her mouth was open. Her eyes were blank. If this was her happy face, Emily didn't ever want to be around when she heard bad news.

"Whatever's the matter with you?" Dr. Muriel asked her. "You look as though you've seen a ghost."

Miranda took a deep, calming breath and exhaled slowly. "I talked to the head teacher. She just checked the classroom, and... Sophie's there."

"So this isn't Sophie?"

"Unless she can be in two places at once," said Ray.

"Whoa!" said Selena. "Teleportation?"

Sophie smiled, innocently enough. But maybe the smile was a little... otherworldly.

"What *is* your name, dear?" asked Dr. Muriel.

"Sophie."

Dr. Muriel turned to Emily. "What do you think? Twins, aliens, ghosts, magic, teleportation?"

"Miranda said that a lot of the illusions inside the forest are simple things dressed up to look more complex. I think something like that has happened here."

"You better come up with something quick," said Ray. "The police'll be here in"—he checked his watch—"about eight minutes."

"OK. Let's start from the beginning. Harry told me he doesn't see his granddaughter very often. Her name's Sophie. She goes to a school not far from where we live. Harry got permission to take her out of school to bring her here to test the magical forest. He brought her here on the bus. I saw them both when they arrived. You guided them through the forest, Ray. They stopped and saw Santa, had their photo taken. When they came out of the forest to collect Sophie's gift, Harry thought his granddaughter looked different."

"As though she'd been transformed," said Miranda.

"What if we're all affected?" Selena made a nervous, whickering sound. "I'm serious. Who's next?"

Emily shook her head. "Sophie looked exactly the same to me when she came out of the forest as when she went into it. It was only when he put his glasses on that Harry realized she wasn't his granddaughter. Same build, same hair colour, same name. Close, but not quite right."

"Ah," said Dr. Muriel. "How many girls in your class are called Sophie?"

Sophie held up her right hand. She unfurled one finger, two, three.

Emily nodded. "He had gone to the school and told them he had permission to collect a child called Sophie, and they produced a little girl called Sophie—someone's granddaughter. Just not yours, Harry."

Miranda rang Sophie's head teacher, putting her on speakerphone for the benefit of the group.

She sounded frantic. "I can't talk now, Miranda. A child's gone missing at the school."

"About four foot tall, six years old, blonde," Dr. Muriel called out to her. "Name of Sophie? I think we can help with that."

"I'll bring her back on the bus now," said Harry. "If her mother agrees."

"Can you plant my flower with me?" Sophie asked him.

"If your mother agrees."

"You know, you got your Christmas wish," Emily said to Miranda, when the logistics for returning Sophie to the school had been agreed with the head teacher. "For a while, people really did think the magic in the forest might be real. Or Selena and Ray did, anyway."

"I didn't!" protested Ray.

"I did," said Selena. "I really did."

"And you got your puzzle," said Miranda to Emily.

Emily grinned at her. "As always."

"But I still haven't got a granddad," said Sophie. For the first time that day, she looked as though she might cry.

"Well, I can't say for certain," said Emily, "but Harry looks like a granddad to me. He *acts* like a granddad, travelling on the bus with you and offering to help you plant your amaryllis. So..."

"Yes," said Sophie, cheering up. She put her hand in Harry's. "He must be real."

"Did you notice how Selina seemed to get a bit more centaur-like, the more time she spent in the forest?" Emily asked Dr. Muriel.

"There was a good bit of whinnying," admitted Dr. Muriel. "And pawing the ground. Wasn't she doing that at the beginning?"

"No! Ray became more heroic. Harry got to spend time with Sophie. Sophie got her Grandad. Miranda got her wish. I got my puzzle. It almost makes me believe in magic."

"Ha!" said Dr. Muriel. "Almost."

From out of the corner of her eye, Emily saw a small reindeer emerge from the forest and run across the room.

By the same author:

THE EMILY CASTLES MYSTERIES

Invitation to Die is a quintessentially English murder mystery featuring an astutely drawn mix of larger-than-life characters... The book is very funny indeed... There seems to be a winning line on every page.

*The bookbag.co.uk*

An intelligent, likeable contemporary heroine and a clever plotline... Like a modern day Agatha Christie.

*Just a Normal Girl in London*

Quirky, whimsical, smart, and engaging... I flat-out loved it. A must-read for romance readers.

*Connie Brockway, bestselling romance author and two-time RITA award-winner*

I love Helen Smith's writing. Her brand of mystery, shot through with clever observational humour and the sharpest of wit, is something that's been missing from the genre for far too long.

*Alex Marwood, Edgar award-winning author of The Wicked Girls*

Entertaining, gripping and fast paced with laugh-out loud moments.
*Bookfabulous*

This book is full of great lines, I was giggling through the book.
*Wall-to-Wall Books*

Invitation to Die is a fast, funny, easy read with many enjoyable comic moments.
*Mystery People*

All crime fiction readers will find this a quick and fun read. Fans of MC Beaton's Agatha Raisin or Simon Brett's Mrs Pargeter series will enjoy the humour and slightly surreal quality of this novel.
*Crime Fiction Lover*

Delightful stuff.
*Shots Magazine*

By the same author:

ALISON WONDERLAND
Only occasionally does a piece of fiction leap out and demand immediate cult status. Alison Wonderland is one.
*The Times*

Smith is gin-and-tonic funny.
*Booklist*

BEING LIGHT
Smith has a keen eye for material details, but her prose is lucid and uncluttered by heavy description. Imagine a satire on Cool Britannia made by the Coen Brothers.
*Times Literary Supplement*

This is a novel in which the ordinary and the unusual are constantly juxtaposed in various idiosyncratic characters... Its airy quirkiness is a delight.
*The Times*

THE MIRACLE INSPECTOR

The Miracle Inspector is one of the few novels that everyone should read, it's a powerful novel that's masterfully written and subtly complex.
*SciFi and Fantasy Books*

Helen Smith crafts a story like she's the British lovechild of Kurt Vonnegut and Philip K. Dick.
*Journal of Always Reviews*

About the author:

Helen Smith is a novelist and playwright who lives in London. She is the author of *Alison Wonderland, Being Light* and *The Miracle Inspector* as well as the Emily Castles mysteries.

61746259R00032

Made in the USA
Lexington, KY
02 April 2017